Buster's New Friend

A Marc Brown ARTHUR Chapter Book

Buster's New Friend

Text by Stephen Krensky
Based on a teleplay by Matt Steinglass

L|B
1837

Little, Brown and Company
Boston   New York   London

First Edition

The characters and events portrayed in this book are fictitious. Any similarity to real persons, living or dead, is coincidental and not intended by the author.

Arthur® is a registered trademark of Marc Brown.

Text has been reviewed and assigned a reading level by Laurel S. Ernst, M.A., Teachers College, Columbia University, New York, New York; reading specialist, Chappaqua, New York.

Library of Congress Cataloging-in-Publication Data

Krensky, Stephen.
    Buster's new friend / text by Stephen Krensky ; based on a teleplay by Matt Steinglass. — 1st ed.
        p. cm. — (A Marc Brown Arthur chapter book ; 23)
    Summary: Arthur's feelings are hurt when Buster begins to spend all his time with his new friend, Mike.
    ISBN 0-316-12212-2 (hc) / ISBN 0-316-12307-2 (pb)
    [1. Aardvark — Fiction. 2. Animals — Fiction. 3. Friendship — Fiction.] I. Title.
PZ7.K883 Bv 2000
[Fic] — dc21   00-030146

10 9 8 7 6 5 4 3 2

LAKE (hc)
COM-MO (pb)

Printed in the United States of America

For Miles Criffield, F.C.N.:
First-Class Nephew

Chapter 1

. . . .

Arthur was sprawled on the rug in the den playing with two horseshoe magnets. If he touched their ends together one way, the magnets stuck together. But if he flipped one over, then the ends repelled each other.

His sister D.W. came in and turned on the TV.

"D.W., can't you see I'm working?"

"But, Arthur, it's time."

"*Up next,*" said the TV announcer, "*it's a half hour of action-packed thrills with Earth's mightiest superhero — Bionic Bunny!*"

1

"Oh, sorry," said Arthur. "I didn't realize it was that late."

A key zipped out from under the couch and stuck to one of the magnets.

"Did you see that?" asked D.W. "It was magic."

"Not magic," said Arthur. "Magnetism. An invisible force that attracts metal objects together."

"That's what I said. Magic."

Arthur sighed. "Anyway, don't touch these magnets. They're for the science project I'm doing with Buster. He's coming over to watch *Bionic Bunny,* and then we're going to work together."

"Can I help? I'll bet I could be good at magic."

"No, you can't. You're too young."

D.W. made a face.

"But you can watch *Bionic Bunny* with us," Arthur added.

"Okay." D.W. looked out the window.

"Why isn't Buster here already? *Bionic Bunny* is about to start."

"He'll be here," said Arthur. "He always makes it in time."

But not that day. The show opened as Bionic Bunny raced through the sky trying to stop a missile from exploding.

"Must . . . stop . . . missile!" he said, straining every muscle in his bionic body.

D.W. tugged Arthur's sleeve. "Maybe Buster doesn't like *Bionic Bunny* anymore."

"Don't be silly," said Arthur. "Buster's just running a little late."

A half hour later, the show concluded with the president congratulating Bionic Bunny on the White House lawn.

"You're a credit to the country," said the president.

Bionic Bunny stared at the grass. *"I do the best I can, sir,"* he said.

"Thanks for saving the free world," the president went on.

"But . . . who are you, really?" asked a nearby reporter.

"Just a citizen trying to do his duty," Bionic Bunny insisted, flying into the sunset as the credits started to roll.

Arthur clicked off the TV, frowning. There was still no sign of Buster. How could they do the project together if Buster wasn't there?

"Buster missed the whole episode," said D.W.

"I know that, D.W.," said Arthur. "Something must have happened. Maybe something terrible."

Arthur went to the telephone. He called Buster's mother at work.

"Hello, Mrs. Baxter? This is Arthur. I've been waiting a long time for Buster, but he's not here. I think he's missing. . . . He's not? He's where?" Arthur frowned. "Oh, I see. Well, thanks. Sorry to bother you. Bye."

Arthur hung up.

"So where is he?" asked D.W.

"He's out playing miniature golf."

"Why didn't he invite you?"

"Mrs. Baxter said he's playing with his new friend, Mike."

"Mike?" D.W. frowned. "Who's Mike?"

Arthur had no idea.

Chapter 2

• • • • • • • • • • •

The next morning, Arthur met Buster at their usual corner on the way to school. Buster wasn't moving too fast, because he was hitting a golf ball with a stick as he walked.

"Steady," Buster mumbled to himself. "Steady . . ."

"Buster?"

"Oh, hi, Arthur." Buster picked up the ball and put it in his pocket. "I was just practicing. Yesterday I went mini-golfing with my new friend, Mike."

"So that's where you were. Don't you know you missed *Bionic Bunny?*"

Buster shrugged. "It's only a cartoon, Arthur. And I'll bet we've seen it before."

"Well, yes, but —"

"Did I tell you that Mike got a hole-in-one on the fourteenth hole? Hardly anyone ever does that. It has a water hazard."

"Mike? Who's Mike?"

Buster bragged, "Just the best mini-golfer I've ever seen. You should see how he judges the slope of the turf. He kneels down and everything."

"Is that important?"

"Of course!"

Arthur frowned. "Well, in case you've forgotten, we were supposed to —"

"I know, I know," said Buster.

"You do?"

"I shouldn't just talk about the mini-golf. There's a lot more to Mike than that. He has tons of amazing CDs. He knows the lines from all the old movies. Everyone who knows Mike thinks he's really cool."

Just over the horizon, a boy in a leather jacket and sunglasses was riding his mountain bike down the road.

Buster was riding beside him. They pulled up to the mini-golf course and were immediately surrounded by their fans.

"It's Mike!"

"And Buster!"

"I think I'm going to faint!"

Everyone herded closer, hoping to get an autograph. Arthur was stuck at the back, but he tried to inch forward.

"Excuse me, coming through! Excuse me!"

An angry fan turned to him. "No pushing! You have to wait your turn just like the rest of us."

"But I know them," said Arthur. "Buster and I have been friends for years."

"Yeah, right! Then why are you stuck back here?"

Arthur didn't have a good answer. "Please, please . . . I must get closer."

Nobody cared. Far ahead Mike and Buster were swept away by a sea of well-wishers, and Arthur was left behind.

"So what do you think?" Buster asked.

Arthur blinked. Somehow they had arrived at school. "What do I think of what?" he asked.

"Of Mike, silly. I've been telling you all about him."

"Um, he sounds terrific. Maybe the three of us could do something together."

Buster beamed. "That's a great idea. I'm sure Mike could help us out on our science project."

"So you do remember!"

"Naturally."

"Well, I've been doing a lot of research. And I think the best —"

"We'll ask Mike what to do," said

Buster. "I'll bet he knows a lot about scientific stuff."

"Okay," said Arthur. "Sure. Bring him by after school."

"We'll be there!" said Buster.

They went inside.

Chapter 3

• • • • • • • • • • • •

That afternoon, Arthur sat at his desk inspecting all the materials for his science project. He had magnets in different shapes and sizes and lots of metal washers, paper clips, nails, and screws.

Arthur was looking through a book, *Sticking Together: Magnetism Through the Ages,* when there was a knock at the door.

"Come in," said Arthur.

He was expecting Buster and Mike, but it was his mother instead. She was carrying a tray with three glasses of juice and a bowl of popcorn.

"I brought up a snack for you and your friends."

"Thanks, Mom. I'm sure they'll be here any minute."

Mrs. Read put down the tray.

"Have a good time," she said, "and don't work too hard." Then she left.

For a few more minutes, Arthur sat waiting for Buster and Mike to show up. Finally, he took a sip of juice and a handful of popcorn.

"I guess I should get started without them," he said to himself.

An hour later, the three glasses were empty and so was the bowl.

"So," said Arthur, reading aloud, "if the magnetic field goes out sideways from the poles of the magnet . . ."

He had tested all of the metal objects on the desk and had taken three pages of notes on which ones stuck to the magnet.

"Arthur?" said Mrs. Read, sticking her head through the doorway.

"Yes, Mom?"

His mother looked around. "What happened to Buster and Mike?"

"I, um, guess they must have forgotten."

"Oh, dear. That isn't like Buster. Well, I'm sure he had a good reason. Anyway, dinner's in a few minutes."

"Okay." He glanced at the empty bowl and glasses. "I'm not that hungry, but I'll be down."

After she left, Arthur stared at his magnets — and then knocked them all over. "Yeah," he said, "I'll just bet they forgot."

Arthur was standing at the door of a laboratory gleaming with stainless-steel tables. All along one wall was a bank of computers, their lights flashing furiously.

In the middle of the room, a figure in a white lab coat stood at a long bench. His back was to Arthur, so Arthur couldn't tell who he was.

But Arthur did recognize Buster, who was strapped to the bench itself. He was struggling to get free.

"Your efforts are useless," said the figure. "You are in my power."

"Never," said Buster. "I will not give in to you. My will has the strength of a thousand butterflies."

"Butterflies don't have much strength," the figure pointed out.

"Don't forget, I said a thousand of them. That should count for something."

The figure cackled loudly. "Have you forgotten? I am Dr. Mike. Your will is putty in my hands." He took out a shiny watch and swung it in front of Buster's face.

"That old trick?" said Buster. "I've seen a lot of old movies. I'm not falling for that."

Dr. Mike swung the watch back and forth, back and forth.

"Repeat after me. I will not go to Arthur's house," said Dr. Mike.

Buster's face suddenly went blank. "I will not go to Arthur's house," he repeated.

"I will never visit Arthur's house again," said Dr. Mike.

"I will never visit Arthur's house again," said Buster.

Arthur tried to call out and rush to Buster, but his voice didn't work. And his feet felt like they were nailed to the floor.

Dr. Mike cackled again, and Arthur shuddered. There was nothing he could do. He was powerless.

Chapter 4

· · · · · · · · · · ·

At lunch the next day, Arthur sat eating his sandwich in the cafeteria. Francine, Muffy, and the Brain were sitting there, too. But if any of them had suddenly asked Arthur what he was eating, he wouldn't have been able to say. His mind was on other things.

"Earth to Arthur," said Francine. "Come in, Arthur."

"Huh?" Arthur sat up. "Sorry, I was just wondering where Buster is. He never seems to be around anymore."

Francine crossed her arms angrily. "Tell me about it! Yesterday, we had a baseball game all planned. I was counting on him to be my catcher. But he never showed up."

"That's nothing," said Muffy from the other end of the table. "You know how Buster's such an expert on bikes? Well, he was supposed to meet me at the bike store to help me pick out a new one. But he never got there. I waited and waited and waited."

"So what did you do?" asked Arthur.

"The only thing I could do," said Muffy. "I had to buy them all."

Arthur and Francine shook their heads.

"I recently had a similar experience involving Buster," the Brain admitted. "We had arranged to play Space Fighter Nine over the Internet. At a crucial moment, when I was facing a squadron of enemy fighters, I was counting on Buster to be my wing man. But he wasn't there. I had to face them alone."

"What happened?" asked Arthur.

The Brain looked down. "It wasn't pretty, I can tell you that."

"The point is," said Francine, "what are we going to do about it? We can't just let Buster keep treating us like this."

"Maybe he needs the silent treatment," said Muffy.

"I don't know," said Francine. "The silent treatment is pretty harsh."

"True," said Arthur, "but Buster needs to learn what it feels like to be ignored. Let's try it."

A few moments later, Buster arrived with his tray. "Boy, that food line is long! I'm starved. I barely had any dinner last night. Mike and I went bowling, and I only had time for a burger and a shake!"

The other kids turned away as Buster took a bite of his sandwich.

"Oh," Buster went on, "and Mike taught me all these great tricks. Did you know

that if you spin the ball sideways, it knocks over more pins? Of course, you have to be pretty strong, the way Mike is, to bowl like that."

Arthur checked his sweater for lint while Francine and Muffy inspected the ceiling.

"Tonight, Mike and I are going to this great science-fiction movie he told me about. Everyone gets eaten by plants from outer space." Buster took the last bite of his sandwich. "I can't believe I finished that so fast. I'm still hungry. I'm going to get some more."

Buster got up and left. Francine watched him leave.

"Well, we sure taught him a lesson," she said, sighing.

Arthur frowned. "I think we're going to need to take more drastic action."

Chapter 5

· · · · · · · · · · · ·

After lunch, everyone returned to class. Arthur hadn't figured out a way to get through to Buster, but he wasn't ready to give up yet. It just wasn't right for Buster to treat his friends this way. He needed to be taught a lesson.

"Hey, Arthur!"

Arthur frowned as Buster came up to him.

"I guess we have to give a progress report on that science project today, huh?"

Arthur glared at him.

"Magnets are such a great thing to do a

project on," Buster continued. "I bet we'll have the best project in class."

Arthur kept on glaring.

At the science fair, Arthur showed a large horseshoe magnet suspended from a chain on the ceiling. Buster stood under it in a suit of armor.

"Every magnet has a north and a south pole," he told the assembled students and teachers. "As you will see, north poles attract south poles, and south poles attract north poles."

He threw a switch activating the magnet, and Buster was lifted off the floor.

The crowd applauded.

"But what if I have a more powerful magnet?" asked a voice from the back.

Mike entered dressed as a wizard. Arthur could not make out his face under his huge hat and flowing beard. But he was holding a much bigger magnet than Arthur's. He held it out and pulled Buster toward him.

"And what's more," said Mike the wizard, *"our two magnets repel each other. But since mine is bigger . . ."*

"Aieeeee!" cried Arthur as he was repelled across the room and out the door.

"Arthur?" said Buster.

"What?" Arthur snapped.

Buster retreated a step. "I was wondering what you think our project should be, exactly? I mean, we haven't done much work on it yet."

"Speak for yourself!" said Arthur. "I've done plenty — while you were out bowling with Mike!"

"You have?" Buster reddened.

"We were supposed to get together, *the three of us.* Remember?"

"Well, I . . ."

"But I went ahead on my own. Why don't you go make your own project? I don't want to work with you anymore."

"But . . . but Arthur, I . . . we have to give a progress report."

"Why don't you talk about mini-golf or bowling?" said Arthur. "You're prepared for that."

Mr. Ratburn called for everyone's attention. "I'm sure you've all been working very hard on your science projects. . . ."

The classroom quieted down.

"As you may recall, I'd like each of you to describe your project and what you've done so far. Who should we start with? Let's see. . . . How about you, Buster?"

Buster scratched his ear. "Well, I really don't know where to begin."

"At the beginning would be fine," said Mr. Ratburn.

Buster hesitated. "The truth is, I don't really know what I'm doing."

Mr. Ratburn did not look pleased. "I see, Buster. Haven't I been clear about the need

to get your project under way? I believe I have. Perhaps you and I should have a talk after school."

Buster's eyes looked down at his desk, and then stayed there throughout most of the progress reports.

Chapter 6

• • • • • • • • • • •

Plunk!

Arthur dropped a book into a cardboard box on his bed.

Thud!

A baseball landed next to the book.

Splat!

Three comic books landed on top of the baseball and book.

The propellers on the plane had started turning. Arthur was about to board when he heard a voice.

"So you are giving up, eh?" *said a voice in the shadows behind him.*

"You win, Mike," *said Arthur.* "I won't

stand in Buster's way if he wants a new best friend."

Mike folded his arms. "And what did Buster say when you told him?"

"I didn't," said Arthur. "It's better this way. Besides, you'll think of the right words. You think of everything."

"What are you doing?"

D.W. asked this question as she watched Arthur from the doorway.

"What does it look like?" asked Arthur.

"It looks like you're packing."

Arthur sighed. "I guess I am, in a way."

D.W. gasped. "Are you moving? Can I have your room?"

Arthur took down a Bionic Bunny poster and rolled it up. "I'm not moving, D.W."

His sister looked disappointed. "You're not cleaning, are you? Because if you are, I don't think you're doing a very good job."

Arthur picked up a broken pencil. It was

the pencil he and Buster had used last summer to write a story about the adventures of Super Pal. "No, I'm not cleaning. At least, not the way you mean. I'm just throwing out everything in my room that belongs to Buster, or reminds me of Buster, or has anything to do with Buster."

"Oh. You must be pretty mad."

"You could say that."

D.W. nodded. "Did you and Buster have a fight?"

Arthur shook his head. "No. But he's made it very clear how he feels about me."

D.W. thought for a moment. "Are you going to throw out the radio he gave you when he got that new one for his birthday?"

Arthur looked at the radio. He had been very excited when Buster gave it to him. He had listened to it many times, especially to hear baseball games at night. But

Arthur knew that if Buster had the radio back, he'd give it to his new best friend, Mike.

So Arthur put the radio in the box. "I think that's everything," he said, taking a last look around.

"What about the CDs you borrowed from him?"

Arthur stared at her. "D.W., don't you have something better to do?"

"Not really."

"Well, just leave me alone. Please. The sooner you're gone, the sooner I can get rid of this stuff."

D.W. frowned. "Um, Arthur, that wouldn't be right."

"Why not?"

"Even if you're mad at Buster, these things belong to him. You can't just throw them out. You should give them back."

Arthur groaned — but he knew D.W.

was right. He would bring the box right over to Buster's. And if he was lucky, nobody would be home when he dropped it off.

Chapter 7

• • • • • • • • • • •

Arthur was carrying the box slowly down the street. It was a pretty long way to Buster's house, but Arthur hadn't asked for a ride. His parents would have had questions for sure, and right then Arthur didn't feel like giving the answers.

D.W. had offered to help, but Arthur didn't want company, either. This was something he needed to do alone.

The box didn't seem too heavy at first. Arthur shifted its weight a few times, but it wasn't the box that was weighing him down. It was the memories inside it.

Arthur thought about all the good times he and Buster had shared over the years. He remembered snowball fights and studying for tests and going out on Halloween. He couldn't remember a moment when Buster hadn't been his friend. They had shared so much together. How could Buster forget about him just because he had met someone else?

As Arthur reached the halfway point, his arms began to ache.

"Maybe this wasn't such a good idea," he said to himself, and put the box down to rest.

"Isn't it exciting?" Francine was saying. "Imagine, Buster coming back to our school for a visit."

"I bought a whole new outfit," said Muffy. "I can't wait."

"This is Buster we're talking about," said Arthur. "He doesn't care about those things."

"Maybe the old Buster didn't," said Muffy. "But ever since he and Mike teamed up to make that magnetic car, things have changed."

"I heard he's a millionaire now," said Francine.

"More like a billionaire!" cried Muffy. "Oh, look! Here he comes now!"

A state police motorcycle escort flanked a long, black limousine that was pulling up to the front door. As the car came to a halt, two men in dark suits and sunglasses popped out.

"Perimeter secured," said one, talking into his sleeve.

The other opened the back door.

"I'll just be a minute, Mike," said Buster, stepping out.

The whole school crowded around him.

"Welcome back, Mr. Baxter!" said Mr. Ratburn. "We knew you'd make something of yourself. You were always so well prepared for class."

"Thank you, thank you," said Buster.

"Buster, over here!"

Buster's eyes followed the sound of that voice. "Hello," he said. "Do I know you?"

"Know me? Of course you know me. It's Arthur."

Buster stroked his chin. "Arthur . . . Arthur. . . . Should that name ring a bell?"

One of the dark suit guys whispered in Buster's ear.

"Oh, Arthur! Arthur Weed."

"That's Read," said Arthur. "Arthur Read."

"Whatever," said Buster. "Great to see you. Like old times, isn't it?" He paused. "We did have old times, didn't we?"

Arthur nodded.

Buster looked at his watch. "Oh, my! Where does the time go? I don't want to keep the president waiting. Good-bye, all!"

He ducked back into the limousine, which roared off down the street.

"If you can be that way," said Arthur, "so can I." He picked up the box again. "Just five more blocks to go."

Chapter 8

· · · · · · · · · · · ·

Arthur had almost reached Buster's house when he heard his name called out.

"H-hey, Arthur."

It was Buster. He was approaching fast on his skateboard.

Arthur hesitated. He wondered if he should just give the box to Buster and go home. It was his stuff, after all. Let him carry it the rest of the way.

Buster came to a halt.

"It's funny that you should be passing by," said Buster. "I was just coming over to your house. We need to talk."

Arthur sighed. "Are you sure you have

time? I mean, you've been awfully busy lately."

Buster turned a deep shade of red. Even the tips of his ears got pink. "I know, I know. Listen, I'm sorry about the science project. I didn't realize I was . . . letting you down."

Arthur nodded. "How did your talk with Mr. Ratburn go?"

Buster frowned. "He was pretty disappointed. 'You must learn to plan ahead, Mr. Baxter. Do you know the story about the grasshopper and the ant?' "

"Not that one again!"

Buster nodded.

"What did you tell him?" asked Arthur.

"Well, it's a good story," said Buster. "I didn't mind hearing it again. I really like the part where the grasshopper plays the whole time the ant is working. Besides, Mr. Ratburn is very good at the voices."

"About this box . . . ," Arthur began.

"How about I give you a hand?" asked Buster. "We can put it on the skateboard."

"Um, thanks," said Arthur.

"I know I haven't been seeing you that much since I started hanging out with Mike. I'm sorry. You're still my best buddy. But, you know, Mike's my buddy, too."

"I guess I can understand that."

"Good, good. Anyway, I was hoping that maybe we could still work together on the project. I've thought up a lot of ideas."

"You have?"

"Uh-huh. I was thinking that we could magnetize the whole floor of our classroom and then put small magnets in everyone's sneakers. It would be like skating, but more scientific."

Arthur took a moment to consider it. "How were you thinking we would magnetize the floor?" he asked.

Buster shrugged. "Okay, I haven't worked out all the details. But what about

this, then? We magnetize a basketball rim and our basketballs, too. That way, when we shoot we'll never miss."

"Don't you think people would get a little suspicious?"

Buster shook his head. "We'll just say we've been practicing."

Arthur couldn't help smiling. "And what about the fact that basketballs have no metal in them to magnetize?"

Buster frowned. "They absolutely have to have metal?"

"That's how it works."

"All right. Then we'll have to think of something else. But at least I'm trying. Do you want to come in? My mom made cookies and lemonade. They'll get our brains going. I'll even carry your box."

Without waiting for an answer, Buster started down the sidewalk.

Arthur took a deep breath and then ran to catch up.

Chapter 9

• • • • • • • • • • •

"So then whatever metal the magnet is touching turns into a magnet, too."

Arthur pushed two cookies together at Buster's kitchen table to illustrate his point.

"Cool!" said Buster. "So that's how it works. It's amazing the way the magnetic field lines up the atoms like soldiers." He sighed. "I still like my magnetic-floor idea, but oh, well. Anyway, I promise I'll work hard from now on to make the project the best magnet project we've ever done."

Arthur smiled. "That won't be hard. It's

the *only* magnet project we've ever done. Still, I have to admit, it really wasn't the same without you. Bionic handshake?"

"Aw-right!" said Buster, clasping Arthur's hand with his own.

"Oh. Look!" said Arthur. "It's four-thirty."

Buster nodded. "Time for *Bionic Bunny.*"

The show was about a hungry space alien trying to steal the world's vegetable supply. But Bionic Bunny foiled him, although he did let the alien leave with a generous supply of broccoli and spinach.

"Thank you for saving our farms," said a farmer, at the end.

"But who are you, really?" asked a reporter.

"Just someone trying to do the right thing in this mixed-up world," said Bionic Bunny, Arthur, and Buster all together.

As the credits rolled, Buster shut off

the TV. "I guess we should get back to work."

"Now?" said Arthur. "Boy, you really have changed."

"Well, I don't want to hear 'The Grasshopper and the Ant' again anytime soon. But maybe you have to go. . . . You know, you never told me what you were doing with that box."

Arthur wasn't sure what to say. He didn't want to make things up, but he didn't want to hurt Buster's feelings, either. "Oh, um, that's just some stuff I need to get home. Can you help me?"

"Sure thing. We can take the skateboard. Oh, wait! Mike's coming over in a little while."

Arthur had almost forgotten about Mike. "So, we'll meet at last," he said. "The famous Mike, live and in person."

"That's right," said Buster. "Mike's the

best. If we ask nicely, I'm sure he'll give us a ride."

"Buster, will you knock it off? I mean, I can believe this Mike is a great mini-golfer. And, sure, he could be a terrific bowler, too. And I get that everyone thinks he's cool, cooler than the rest of us could ever hope to be. But now you've gone too far."

Buster looked confused. "What do you mean?"

"A car? Come on, Buster. Kids don't own cars — and they don't drive them, either."

"That's true."

"So why are you saying all this stuff about Mike?"

Now it was Buster who didn't know what to say.

Chapter 10

• • • • • • • • • • • •

Buster blinked. "I don't under— oh, there's Mike's horn. Come see for yourself."

They went outside. Arthur saw a convertible waiting at the side of the road. The top was down, but Arthur didn't see anyone sitting in the passenger seat or the back. He only saw the driver. He wasn't a kid, although as grown-ups went, he was on the young side.

"Hi, Mike!" yelled Buster.

"Hey, Buster! What's up?" said the driver, smiling.

"Mike, I want you to meet my best

buddy, Arthur. Arthur, this is my Big Brother, Mike."

"I've heard a lot about you, Arthur."

Arthur looked dazed as he shook Mike's hand.

"You're Buster's Big Brother?"

"That's right. Buster and I are part of the Big Brother/Big Sister program at the community center."

"My mom signed me up," Buster explained. "She thinks I need an older male influence."

"Somehow," said Mike, "Mrs. Baxter isn't convinced that Bionic Bunny can do the job alone."

"You watch the *Bionic Bunny* show?"

"Of course. How can anyone not want to keep track of a guy who just wants *to do the right thing in this mixed-up world?*"

Buster asked Mike if he could give Arthur a ride.

"Sure. Hop in!"

Arthur ran back to get his box. When he returned, Mike helped him in.

"I have to apologize to you, Arthur."

"You do?"

Mike nodded. "I'd show you how to fight dragons or build a spaceship from scratch, but we're a little short on time today."

"I understand," said Arthur, smiling. Buster had sure been right about his new friend. "Um, Mike, can I ask you a question?"

"Sure. Fire away."

"What do you know about magnets?"

"Ah, magnets," said Mike as they pulled away from the curb. "I had to do a big project on them once. . . ."